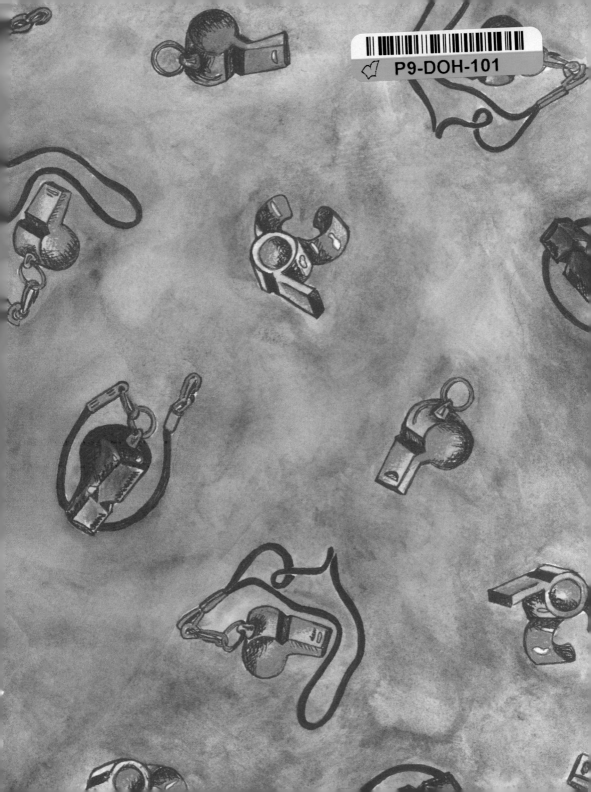

P9-DOH-101

Drop the Puck
It's Hockey Season
THE OFFICIAL ADVENTURES

BOOK 1

Written by Jayne J. Jones Beehler
Illustrated by Katrina G. Dohm

DROP THE PUCK—IT'S HOCKEY SEASON: THE OFFICIAL ADVENTURES © copyright 2016 by Jayne J. Jones Beehler and Katrina G. Dohm. All rights reserved. No part of this book may be reproduced in any form whatsoever, by photography or xerography or by any other means, by broadcast or transmission, by translation into any kind of language, nor by recording electronically or otherwise, without permission in writing from the author, except by a reviewer, who may quote brief passages in critical articles or reviews.

ISBN 13: 978-1-63489-028-1
LCCN: 2016930375
Printed in the United States of America
First Printing: 2015

20 19 18 17 16   6 5 4 3 2

Book design and typesetting by Tiffany Daniels.

WISE Ink
CREATIVE ★ PUBLISHING

Wise Ink Creative Publishing
837 Glenwood Avenue
Minneapolis, MN 55405
wiseinkpub.com

To order, visit www.itascabooks.com or call 1-800-901-3480.
Reseller discounts available.

To the many hockey players in our lives, past and present, who shared their passion, love, and spirit of the game.

A Note from Jayne and Katrina

We promise you will fall in love with this tale of two brothers, Cullen and Blaine. They love hockey and each other. We have included a glossary in the back to help you understand new words in the book and learn more about hockey.

Blaine was born with Down syndrome and has special needs. Down syndrome is a genetic disorder that can cause physical growth delays, characteristic facial features, and mild to moderate intellectual disability.

Blaine's speech, at times, can be stuttering, slurring, and repetitive. It might be challenging to read and understand at first. But don't give up. Blaine wouldn't, and you shouldn't either! As you read, ask your parents and friends if you need help. You can also talk to us at

chris@officialadventures.org.

And the story goes . . .
for the love of the game.

PREGAME
1
Breezers and Jerseys

*I*t was the day after Thanksgiving.
Delicious dinners of turkey and
fixin's were done. For many, it
was a day of shopping and
reminiscing about their traditions
and family gatherings.

Most people's tummies were still full. But anxious and energetic hockey fans had room in their tummies for a few butterflies to flutter. The biggest and best Thanksgiving tradition remained—another reason for giving thanks. It was the holiday tournament and the launch of the long-awaited hockey season!

Rylee the Referee grabbed his cell phone and texted his reffing partner, Rosee the Referee. "U ready to rock it, Ref Rosee? C U at the rink in 10. Don't forget your whistle!" Ref Rylee grabbed his skates, whistle, and bag. He headed out the door.

As the snow fell lightly outside, young skaters tucked their brand-new jerseys into their breezers. They laced up their just-sharpened skates.

And the crisp sound of the puck-drop saluted the start of the season!

Hockey moms and grandmas settled on the bleachers. They were covered head to toe in toasty, warm blankets. They sipped hot chocolate to help keep the chill away.

Proud dads gathered together, greeting each other with high fives and handshakes. Each one tried to outdo the other with noise to show how pumped up they were for their favorite sport.

"The blood's in our g-game, and the g-game's in our blood," sang Blaine as he jammed to his favorite song on his headphones.

Looking at his younger brother, Cullen tried to hide behind his overstuffed hockey bag. "Mom, can't you do something? No one pumps up to 'The State of Hockey' song!" Cullen smiled as he let out a good-natured groan.

"Oh, come on. I think every Minnesota hockey player does! You pump up for games to your favorite song," their mom replied. "You know Blaine is just as fired up as you. We have more than one hockey lover in this family. Blaine might have Down syndrome, but life surely doesn't get him down!"

"Yeah, but Blaine's just the team manager. Filling water

bottles and taping hockey sticks is nothin' like scoring a hat trick every game." Cullen winked.

"He might not be scoring goals on the ice, but he's scoring goals in the game of life!" their mom reminded him.

"Let's play hockey!" celebrated Ref Rylee as he walked into the rink. He hugged Blaine with excitement. "It's great to see you back at the rink, Blaine. I need to go find Rosee, your other favorite referee. Ref Rosee and I will see you on the bench. And don't you even think about squirting me with a water bottle. But squirting Ref Rosee is fair game." Ref Rylee

winked as he walked off with
a grin.

"I g-got a hug from R-Rylee
the Referee," an elated Blaine
bragged to Cullen.

"Settle down, little bro! It's time
to head over to the bench and
get your manager work done. We
need to win this tourney. Hugging
the referee doesn't help score
goals." Cullen laughed.

"N-no. But it might help . . .
k-keep you out of the penalty
box!" joked Blaine.

"Really? In that case, Blaine,
you better go get a hug from
Rosee the Referee too!" Cullen

joked back as the family shared a traditional pregame laugh.

Without skipping a beat, Blaine snapped his headphones back on with a smile on his face. His voice rang out, "Innnn the state, the state of hockey, hockey!"

The sheet of ice glistened. It was resurfaced and ready for hockey. Players huddled up close to the rink boards. They got last-minute words from their coaches as they waited for the referees to join them on the ice.

Cullen looked up to the bleachers. He saw all the parents carefully positioning their cell phones to take photos of the game, the team, and their favorite players.

He thought to himself, "Our best fans are our parents and families." His family didn't miss a game. Half of his mom's pictures would proudly be action shots of Blaine on the bench. Cullen couldn't wait to see what pictures she took today. He wanted to update his social media cover photo and show his friends what they were missing.

PERIOD ONE

2

Whistles

"Yeah! Woot, woot. W-woot!" yelled Blaine. He clapped his hands as Ref Rylee skated by the bench.

Ref Rylee did a quick snow-spraying stop. With a grin, he asked

Blaine, "Hey, man—you ready for this game?"

Nervous to talk, Blaine slurred, "Yes, yes, y-yes, SIR." He organized the team's sticks in order of height and checked the water bottles.

"You are the best hockey manager in America," Ref Rylee praised.

"I know!" Blaine laughed.

Ref Rylee drank from the team's water bottle and then squirted the ice.

"Hey! Watch how much you squirt—I fill those up!" Blaine tried very hard to reply with little slur or interruption. "I love being

the t-team manager. And I love hockey!"

"We all do, Blaine. Best game in the world!" Ref Rylee smiled in agreement.

As Ref Rylee put down the water bottle, Ref Rosee skated over. She picked up the bottle. As fast as Ref Rosee could, she squeezed it at her reffing partner. She gave Ref Rylee a quick shower, which gave Blaine an instant belly laugh.

Blaine's mom was secretly positioned behind the bench with her cell phone. She snapped a quick shot of Blaine laughing at the referees' water fight.

"You ready to get this tournament started?" Ref Rylee asked Blaine. Rylee put his whistle to his mouth.

"I was ready last week! Let's play hockey!" Blaine stated as crisply and proudly as he could.

"You got it, coach." Rylee the Referee winked at Blaine.

Ref Rylee blew his whistle, ordering the face-off. He pointed to both goal judges, readying them for action. He dropped the puck quickly as he skated backward, out of the way.

Instantly, parents began rooting and screaming from the bleachers. There was a bright flash of light on the ice from all the cell phones taking pictures.

Players on each bench joined in with shouts of support.

"Come on, boys! We got to pass the puck," encouraged the coach.

Cullen's team struggled throughout the first period. His team had no shots on goal in the first eight minutes, while the other team had sixteen! Cullen and his teammates were frustrated

and impatient. They all knew
that no offense would mean no
tournament championship trophy.

Blaine clapped louder and
louder in the bench area,

watching every play. As players returned to the bench after each shift, Blaine patted the tops of their helmets as a sign of support.

"Hey, quit smacking our helmets! Leave your hands off my teammates," snapped Cullen. He pointed to the corner of the bench. "Go sit over there!"

Confused by his brother's reaction, Blaine sat quietly on the bench for the rest of the period.

"Knock it off, Cullen," yelled the coach. "Don't take your frustration out on Blaine."

The coach turned to the whole team gathered at the bench. "You all need to start playing the puck. You need to focus on getting goals in the net! We each have a job to do on this team. Blaine is doing his best. He showed up to play and win! Now, the rest of you need to join him and step up and do your job!" Coach said all in one breath.

Cullen knew his coach was right. He realized he took his own frustration out on his brother. But he was still upset. The game wasn't going well at all. Not only was there no offense, but he and his teammates couldn't stay out of the penalty box. The entire team needed to play harder and create scoring chances.

FIRST INTERMISSION

3

Water Bottles

The game was scoreless after
the first period. Blaine quickly
gathered all the water bottles to
fill them. In the locker room, the
team sat quietly.

As Cullen walked in, he slammed his stick against the wall in anger. Instantly the stick snapped, broke into three parts, and flew across the locker room.

"C-cool your j-jets!" Blaine yelled as he went to pick up all of the pieces of the stick.

"Gentlemen . . ." Coach paused and took a breath before he continued. "You have a job to do, and that's to play hockey as a team. Pass the puck, play your positions, and get that puck in the net."

The coach began to walk out

of the locker room. But first, he pointed directly at Cullen. "You owe your parents a hundred dollars for breaking your stick! Get your head back in the game!"

After the last bottle was filled, Blaine roared loudly, "We got this! Go score a g-goal!"

"Get outta here, Blaine!" Cullen burst. He stood up, ordering Blaine to leave the locker room. "You're just the manager—you're not a part of this team!"

The other players didn't say a word. A rare silence fell on the locker room.

Blaine looked confused again. He gathered the water bottles as quickly as he could. With his arms filled to the brim, he walked onto the freshly cleaned ice. Upset and

not thinking, he slipped and fell. The bottles spilled all over.

Blaine's mom saw him fall onto the ice. She stood to go down and help him. As she stepped toward the ice, she saw Ref Rylee skating over to Blaine. She instantly came to a stop as she watched what was taking place on the ice.

"Need a hand?" Ref Rylee kindly asked Blaine.

Blaine shook his head no. He tried not to let Ref Rylee see the tears welling up in his eyes.

Ref Rylee reached out to help Blaine up off the ice, anyway.

"No goals yet in this barn burner," Ref Rylee said. He looked at Blaine and saw the tears. "Hey, what's going on, champ? Cat got your tongue?" he joked as he tried to cheer up Blaine.

"My, my . . . t-team doesn't like me," he answered.

Ref Rylee laughed out loud. When he suddenly realized Blaine was serious, he stopped laughing. He said, "Not a chance, Blaine. You are the heart of this team. You know it, I know it, and they all know it." Ref Rylee pointed to Cullen and the team as they left the locker room. "Chin up, and get back to work," he said to Blaine. "You have a game to win!"

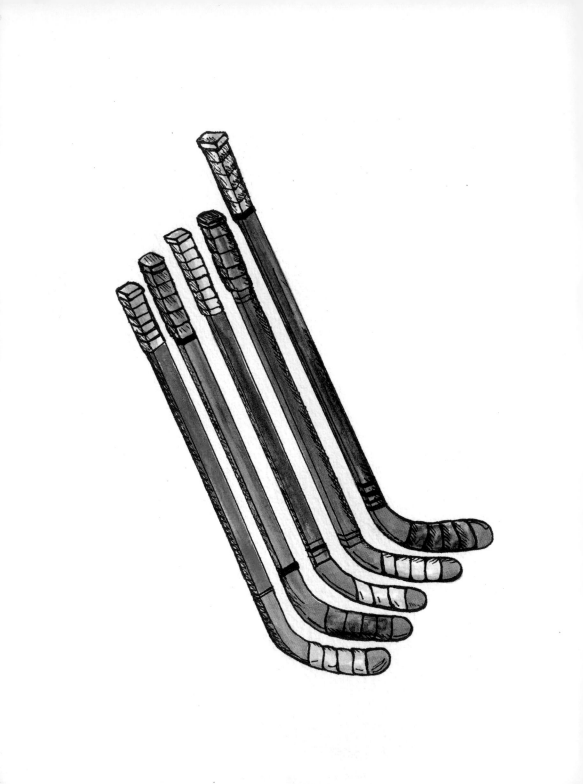

PERIOD TWO

4

Hockey Sticks

Players from both teams took to the ice for the second period. Ref Rylee skated one last circle, passed the team bench, and reached out to give Blaine a high five. But Blaine wasn't on the bench. Ref Rylee saw the team's water bottles lined up perfectly and filled to their brims. In the corner, the team's hockey sticks were taped, ready, and precisely positioned. So where was Blaine?

The second period didn't go much better for Cullen and his team.

Unfortunately, Cullen didn't bring a new attitude onto the ice. Instead, he sat in the penalty box for the majority of the second period. From high-sticking to tripping, Cullen didn't play fair nor was he a good teammate.

His mom took plenty of photos of this record-setting game of penalty minutes.

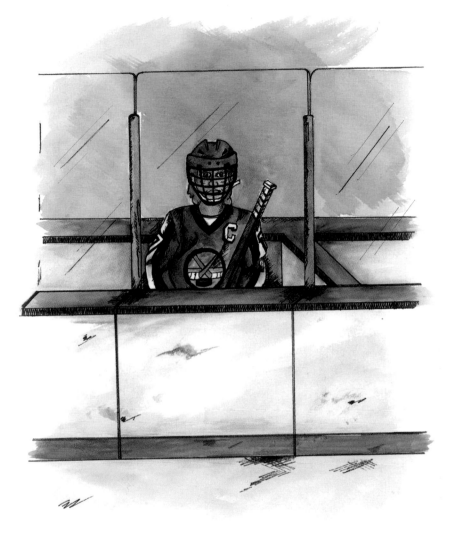

"It might not be the best
memory, but it's certainly a
memory we'll never forget," she
said to his dad as he came up to

the bleachers. "We'll remember it as the Thanksgiving tournament where Cullen sat the entire second period in the penalty box!"

"It takes all kinds of record breakers to make hockey history!" Cullen's grandpa joked.

"Don't go making a hotel reservation for Cullen's induction into the Hockey Hall of Fame just yet!" his mom added with a laugh.

"You gotta love hockey," his dad said. "This game teaches lessons beyond just winning. Speaking of winners, does anyone know where Blaine ran off to?"

"I think he went back into

the locker room," their mom
answered.

The horn blared throughout the
rink. The second period came to
a close. Cullen's team had yet to
score a goal.

FINAL INTERMISSION

5

Paint Cans and Paper

Cullen and his teammates swung their sticks against the ice in frustration and headed to their locker room. As Cullen glided past Ref Rylee, he threw down an empty water bottle and shot it like a puck.

Ref Rylee picked up the water bottle and looked at it closely. The bottle was wrapped with hockey tape. On the tape, a handwritten message read, "The only disability in life is a bad attitude!" Ref Rylee smiled to himself. Blaine wrote that. Ref Rylee wondered if Blaine wrote a message on every bottle.

"Why do we have a team manager if he can't even fill up a water bottle?" Cullen said with obvious frustration.

"The best hockey manager in America wasn't on the bench for the second period," commented Ref Rylee.

"I'm sure my brother is just off pouting," Cullen snapped.

"I don't think he's the one pouting!" Ref Rylee pointed out. "You could learn a lot from Blaine about hockey and life."

"He doesn't know anything about hockey," Cullen shot back as he headed for the locker room, swinging his stick in a hissy fit.

When Cullen kicked open the locker room door, he could not believe his eyes. His teammates couldn't believe their eyes either.

There sat Blaine in the middle of the locker room, surrounded by cans of paint and pieces of poster board.

The team huddled around Blaine
to read his posters. Together, the
posters spelled T-E-A-M.

"Where did you get the paint?"
asked Cullen.

"Mom, b-brought it," answered
Blaine.

The teammates gave Blaine

fist bumps. Genuine smiles and laughter broke out.

"Am I p-part of the team now?" Blaine asked Cullen.

"Part of the team?" Cullen echoed. "You should be wearing this C for captain—not me." Cullen tapped his own chest.

He patted his brother on the head with his gloved hand, just as he would to a teammate. "I'm sorry for being mean to you. Ref Rylee is right on. You are the world's best brother and America's favorite hockey manager!"

"Thanks, Cullen," answered Blaine.

PERIOD THREE

6

Pile of Hats

Ref Rylee skated over just in time to see Cullen patting Blaine's head as they came out of the locker room. "Who's got one last period of hockey in them?" Ref Rylee asked with a grin.

"For the love of the game, we all do!" Cullen stated.

"Best game in the world!" crowed Blaine in agreement. He set up the T-E-A-M posters behind the bench.

46

Ref Rylee looked at the posters and then smiled over at Cullen. "Yep, I think Blaine understands hockey just fine!"

With new spirit, Cullen and his teammates took to the ice. Before long, the horn blared, bringing the third period to a quick close. Cullen had scored a hat trick, and they won their first game of the season!

All the families filed down from the bleachers to take pictures of the team and the final score on the scoreboard.

"That was the most exciting period of hockey I've ever

seen!" yelled Cullen and Blaine's grandpa.

"Where did that sudden spurt of energy and team spirit come from?" questioned their mom.

"I'd like to announce today's player of the game," the coach said as the parents and players gathered around. "Congratulations, Blaine! You didn't give up on the game or give up on the team. Your energy, spirit, and positive attitude shined through and helped us win this game!"

"Way to go, bro! You deserve it!" cheered Cullen. He and the

rest of the team picked Blaine up and lifted him high above their shoulders.

"C-careful . . . you don't want to drop today's . . . MVP!" Blaine giggled.

ASK THE OFFICIALS
Rylee and Rosee's
Referee Resources

Important Words to Learn

assist: An assist in hockey is credited to up to two players of the scoring team who shot, passed, or deflected the puck toward the teammate who scored the goal.

attitude: A feeling or a tendency to respond positively or negatively toward a certain idea, object, person, or situation. Attitude influences your choice of action.

barn burner: An extremely exciting hockey game or competition.

body checking: Knocking an opponent, sometimes against the boards or to the ice, by using the hip or body.

breezers: Pants worn as part of a hockey player's uniform.

championship: A competition held to determine a winner.

Down syndrome: A genetic disorder that can cause physical growth delays, characteristic facial features, and mild to moderate developmental disabilities.

goal: A goal is worth one point in hockey and is valid when a puck passes over the goal line and into the opposing team's goalie net.

hat trick: When one player scores three goals in one game.

hissy fit: A tantrum.

Hockey Hall of Fame: A hockey museum dedicated to celebrating the history of ice hockey. It holds exhibits about players, teams, records, and trophies.

official: The main on-ice referee whose job is to determine penalties and award goals during the game. The official uses hand signals to enforce fair rules of the game.

penalty: A punishment for breaking the rules of the game. Most penalties are enforced and served by a player within the penalty box for a set number of minutes, during which the player cannot participate in play. Penalties are called and enforced by the referee.

penalty box: The area where a player sits to serve the time of a penalty.

resurfaced: To clean dirty, rough ice with an ice machine to make fresh, smooth ice.

stuttering: To speak or utter with an irregular repetition or drawing out of sounds.

MEET JAYNE AND KATRINA

Katrina (left) and Jayne (right)

Jayne J. Jones Beehler wears many helmets, including college professor, lawyer, author, wife, mother, advocate for children with disabilities, and a lifelong hockey fan. She's a former live-in nanny who can never have enough children or chaos around her. She resides in Wisconsin and Florida with her husband, daughter, and their adorable, lovable bulldog, Stanley Cup Beehler.

Katrina G. Dohm was exposed to hockey growing up in Minnesota and Wisconsin, but her true love of the game began when she went to college at the University of North Dakota. For the past twenty-two years, Katrina has dedicated herself to being an art teacher and all the "extras" that go with it. Being a wife, mom, teacher, artist, designer, event planner, school spirit guru, coach, and athletic referee has prepared her for this new adventure of creating and illustrating the Official Adventures series. Katrina currently resides in Wisconsin with her husband.

ACKNOWLEDGEMENTS
A team above all.
Above all a team.

The Official Adventures Series came to life thanks to an all-star team.

The hard work, knowledge, and expertise of veteran players, Angela Wiechmann and Tiffany Daniels in editing and design/layout are greatly appreciated. Up and coming stars, James DePolis and Ally Jacoby, both shared their passions and shined with their contributions in design and photography.

A trillion thanks go to three great hockey families: the Leopolds, the Cullens, and the O'Keefe-Hakstols, who have become huge supporters and fans of Blaine, Cullen, Rylee, and Rosee! Also to Dara Beevas and Wise Ink Creative Publishing who continues to help us keep the OA dream alive.

Much love to our biggest fans, our parents, for teaching us never to go through life without goals and our husbands, for reminding us to have fire in our hearts and ice in our veins. Finally, hugs to a special group of ladies, the best cheerleaders ever!

Look for More
Official Adventures
AVAILABLE NOW!

Drop the Puck, Shoot for the Cup
www.officialadventures.org

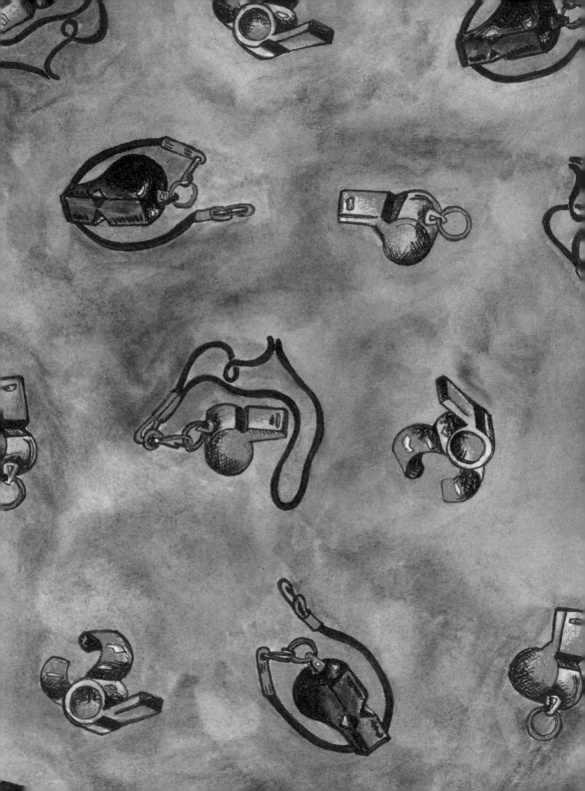